Why Can't We Go to

MARS

FOR A HOLIDAY?

To order additional copies of this book, contact:
Xlibris
AU TFN: 1 800 844 927 (Toll Free inside Australia)
AU Local: 02 8310 8187 (+61 2 8310 8187 from outside Australia)
www.xlibris.com.au
Orders@Xlibris.com.au

ISBN: Softcover   978-1-6698-3036-8
        Hardcover   978-1-6698-3038-2
        EBook   978-1-6698-3037-5

Print information available on the last page

Rev. date: 05/25/2023

Why Can't We Go to

MARS

FOR A HOLIDAY?

JULIA PARKES

Why can't we visit magnificent Mars for our holiday next year?

Because it's dry and dusty, so any photos may not be very clear.

With the lower gravity, we can jump higher here than on Earth.

But we'd have more fun visiting a trampolining centre in Perth!

PERTH

Can we venture to vast Venus for our holiday next year?

No, it's way too hot, as it traps heat in its atmosphere!

We could perhaps see or even experience an active volcano.

But we'd rather watch sea animals play at Sea World in San Diego!

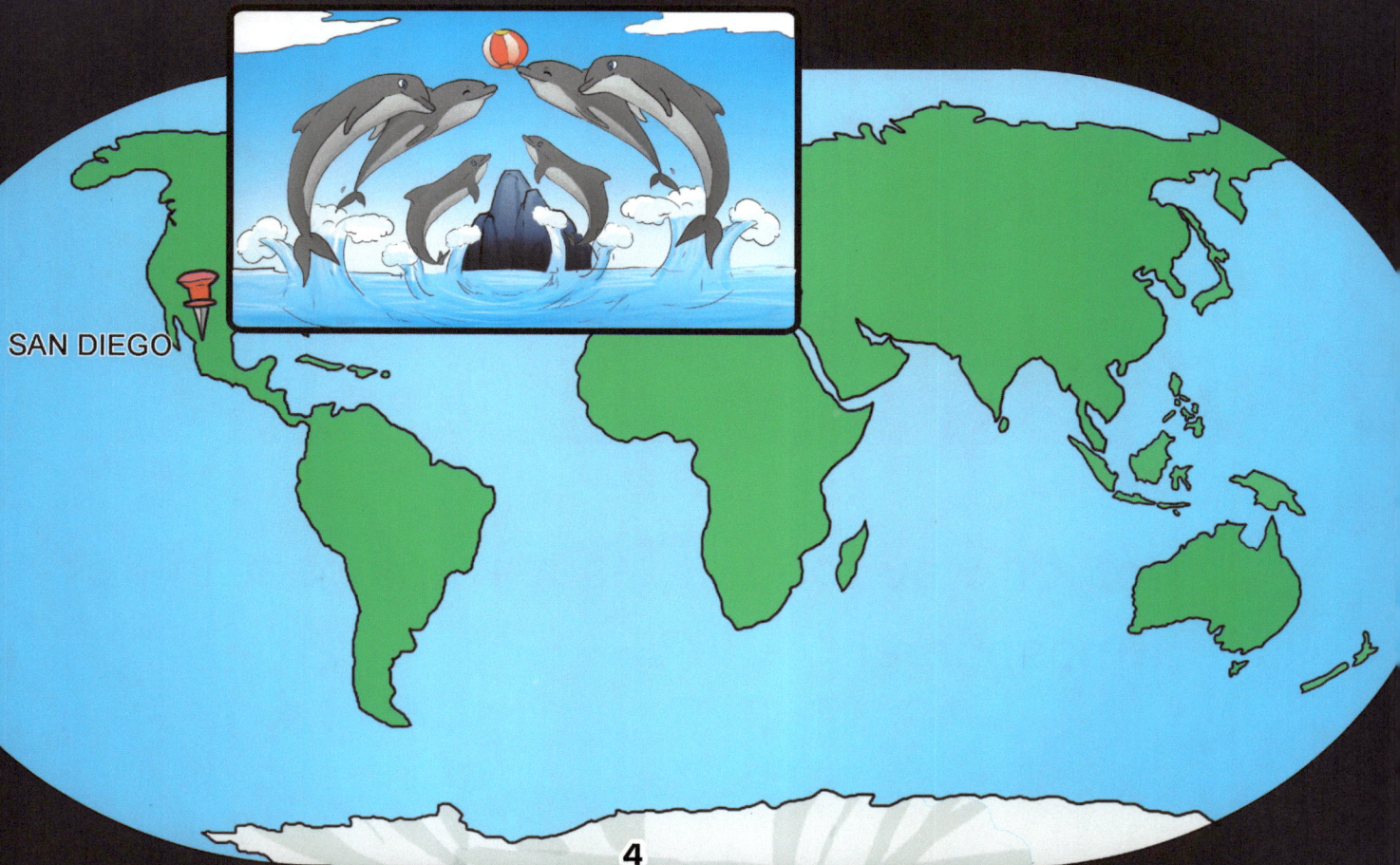

SAN DIEGO

What about the moonless Mercury for our holiday next year?

No, its days are extremely hot, as the sun is so near!

During its very long day, we could explore its many craters.

But we'll be far cooler in a resort pool along the equator!

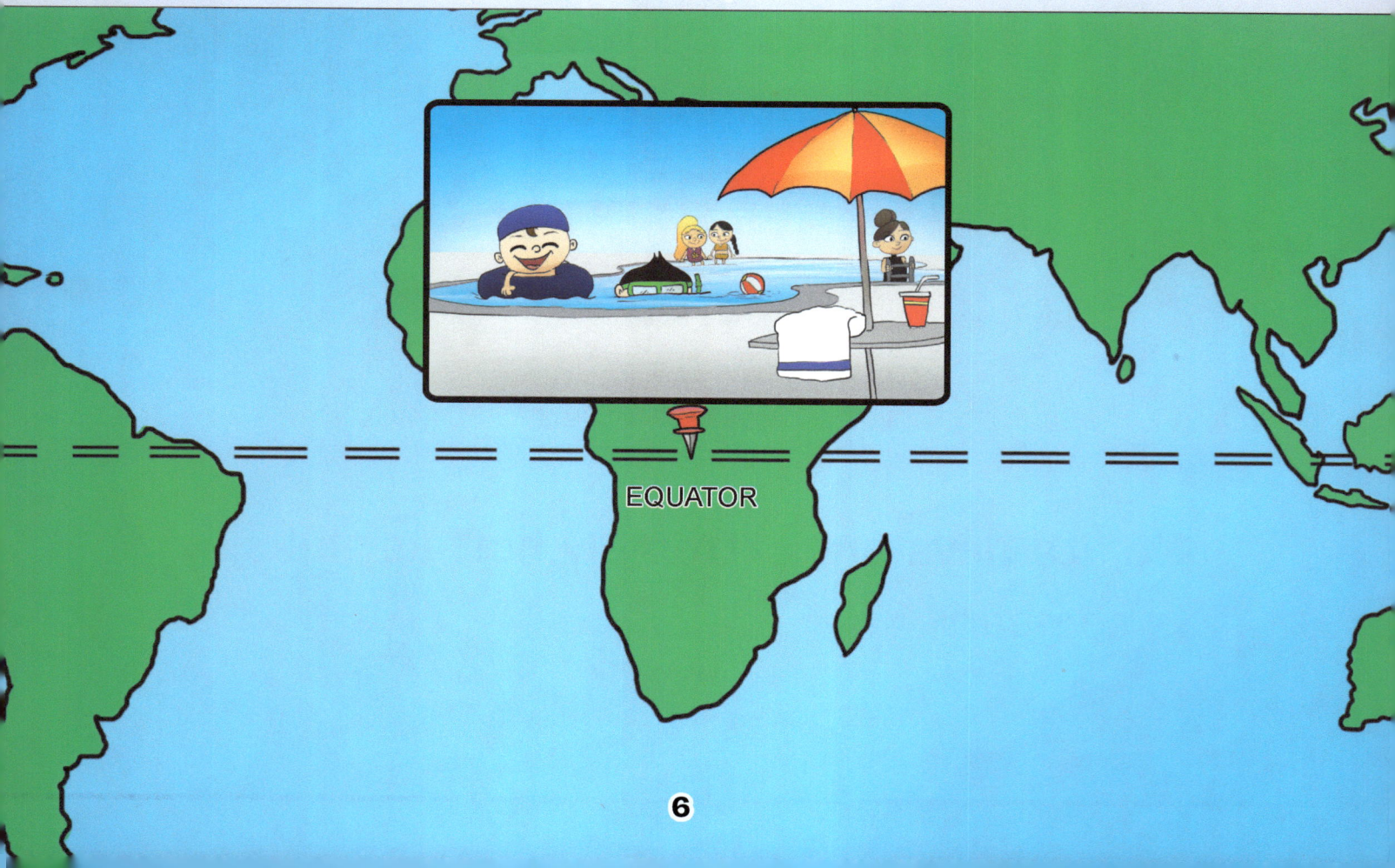

EQUATOR

How about jumbo Jupiter for our holiday next year?

No, we may get caught in a turbulent storm, I fear!

Let's see if its colourful, swirling clouds release some helium rain.

Then again we'll be safer in the rough waters of Maine!

MAINE

May we try the fast-spinning spectacular Saturn for our holiday next year?

Our photos of its beautiful rings will surpass our pictures of the Urangan Pier!

We can't step out onto this planet made of gas for we shall surely fall!

Instead we'll dream of a ride on Canada's highest Ferris wheel in Montreal!

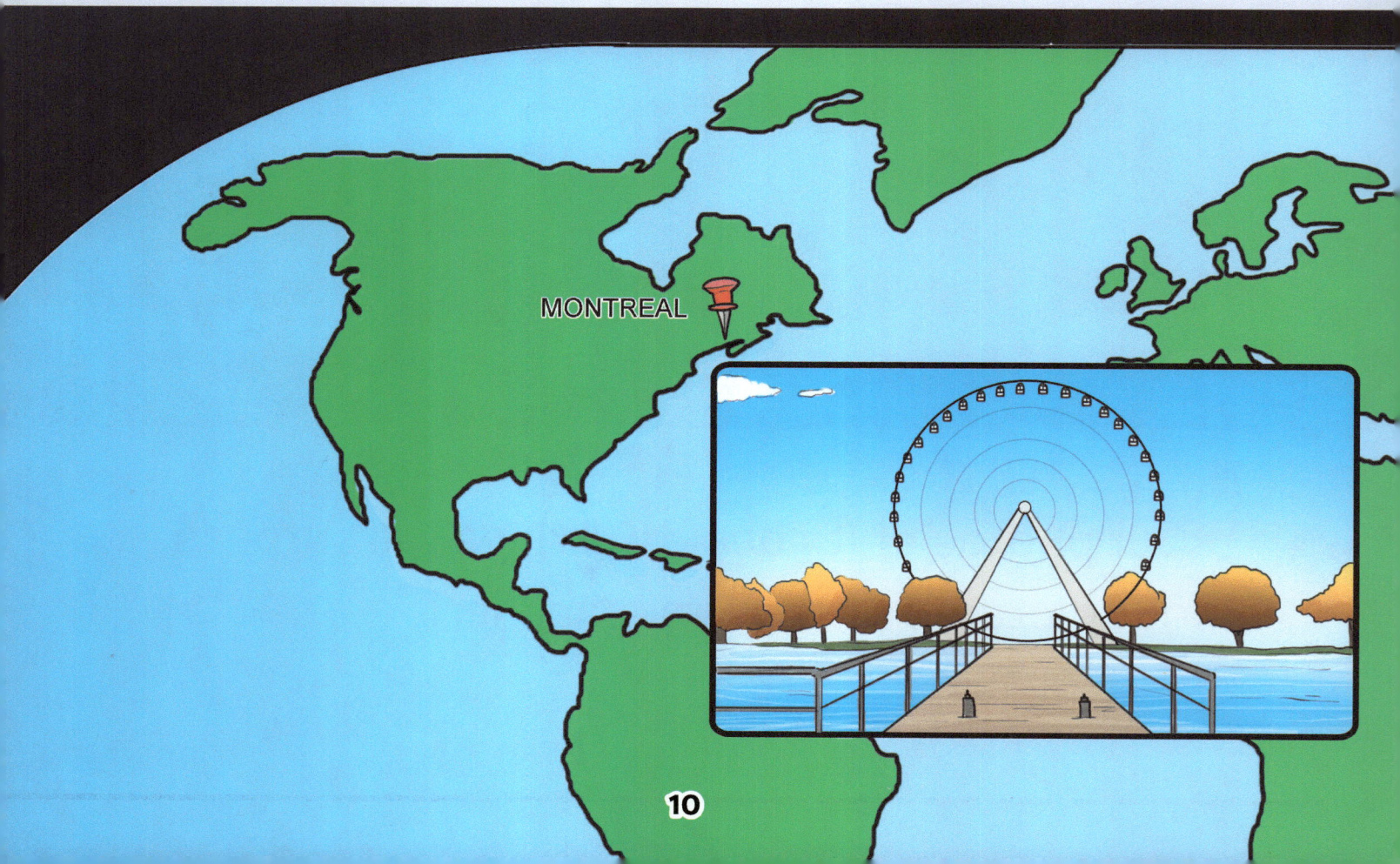

MONTREAL

Can we go to the unique Uranus for our holiday next year?

No, it's an ice giant, and we don't have enough cold weather gear!

Will we visit its south pole pointed to the sun or its dark north pole?

Then again, we could be seeing the palaces, temples, and skyscrapers of Seoul.

SEOUL

Can we visit the distant and nippy Neptune, perhaps, for our holiday next year?

Its powerful winds mean we'll need a specialised driver who can steadily steer!

We could see its special moon, which rotates in the opposite direction, Triton.

Then again, in the cold winds, we'll be yearning for the bay beach at Brighton!

BRIGHTON, VIC

How about the curious Ceres for our holiday next year?

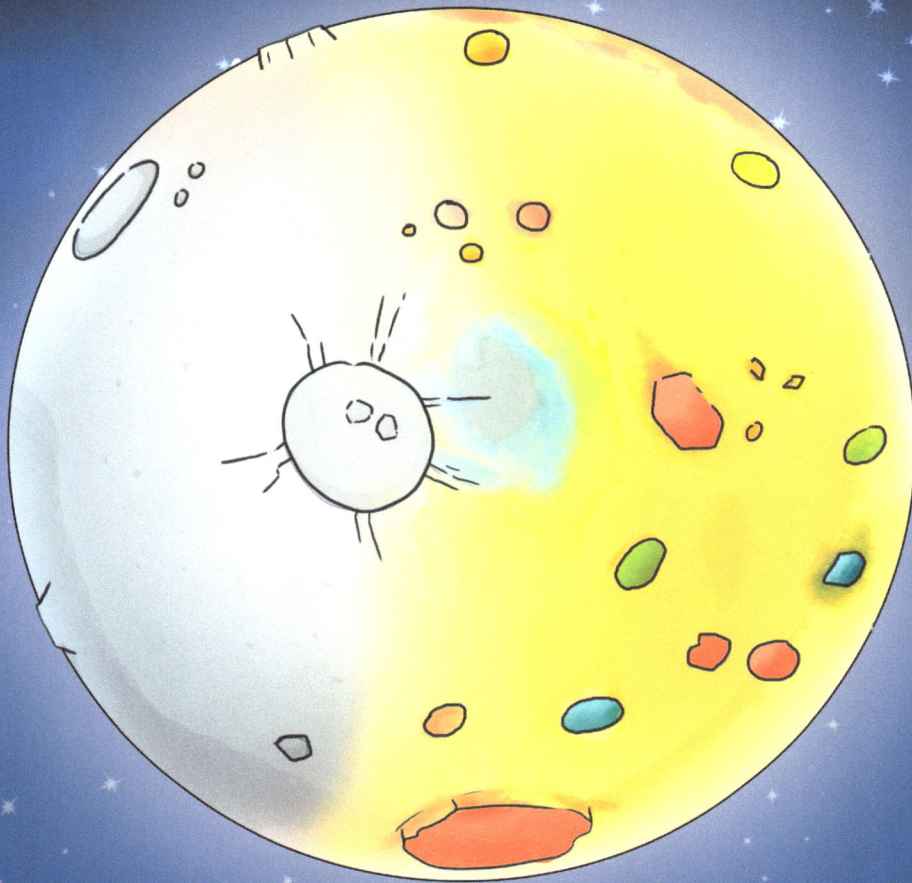

With so much to discover, this will make my science teacher cheer!

Let's see if it has an underground ocean like one of Saturn's icy moons.

However we'd rather be on a sunset camel ride along Cable beach in Broome!

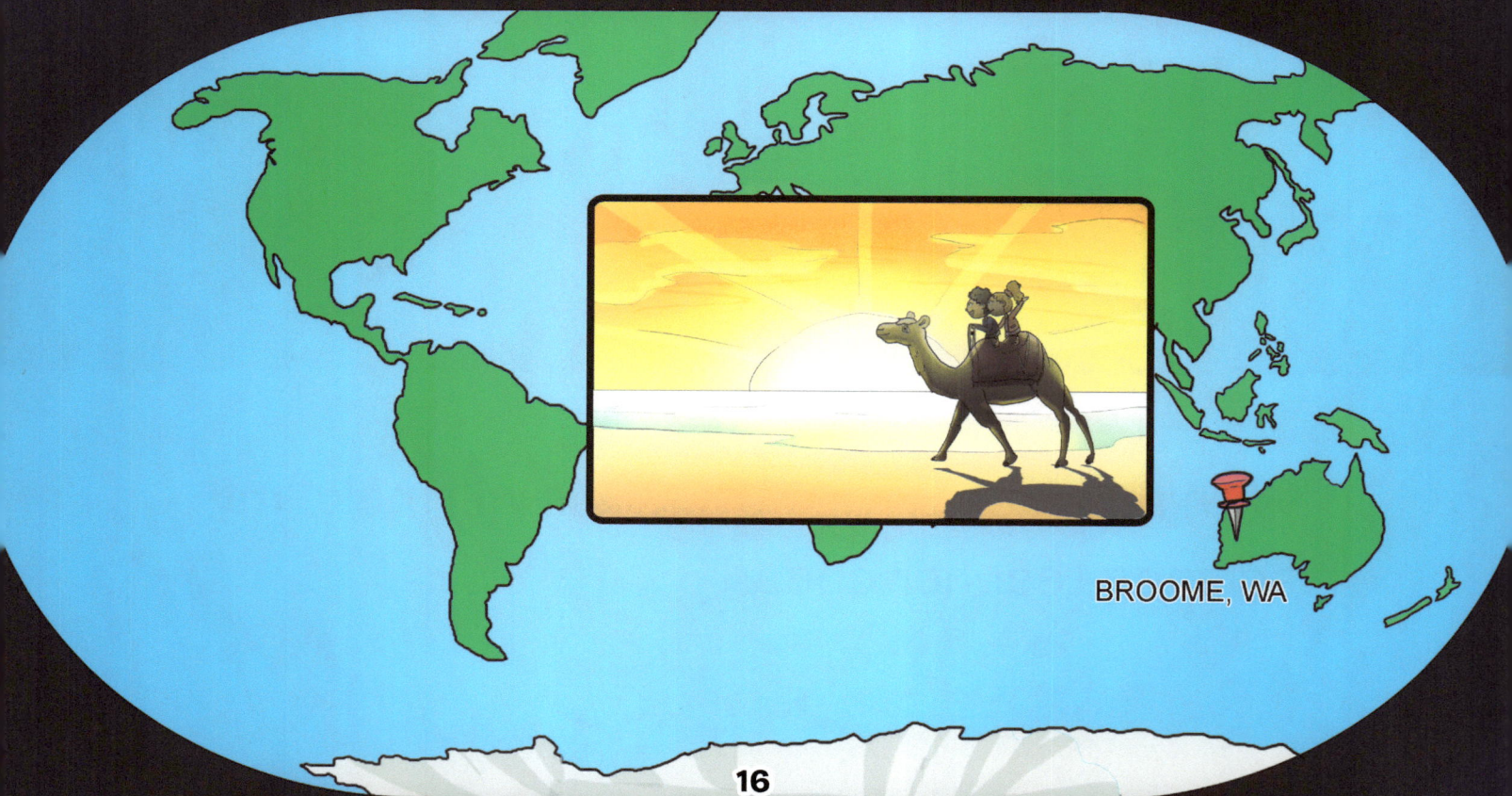

BROOME, WA

What about the phenomenal Pluto for our holiday next year?

No, we'll miss the sound of birds at home that we love to hear!

Let's explore its mountains and valleys and feel its surface of ice and rock.

But we'll soon realise we'll be warmer in one of Scotland's icy lochs.

SCOTLAND

Maybe we could aim for the harsh Haumea for our holiday next year.

This elongated, egg-shaped dwarf planet is so unusual and not a sphere.

We could experience the planet's very short day and very fast spin.

However we may regret not visiting a planetarium or observatory in Berlin!

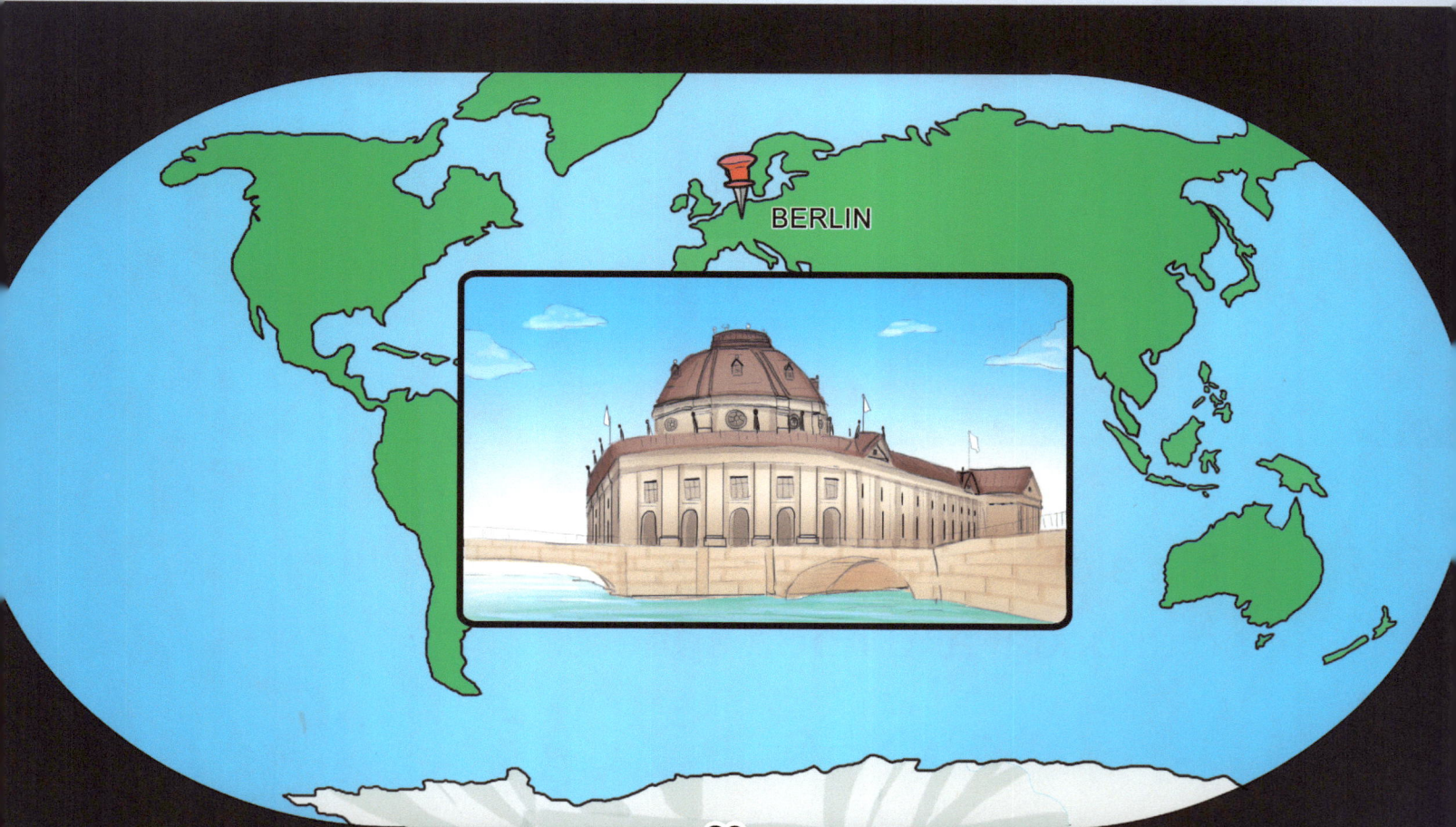

BERLIN

Perhaps we could try the eccentric orbiting Eris for our holiday next year?

Travel to this dwarf planet would enable us to explore an unknown frontier!

It will be a long journey to this icy world from our warm home!

We'll be better off exploring the ancient and great city of Rome!

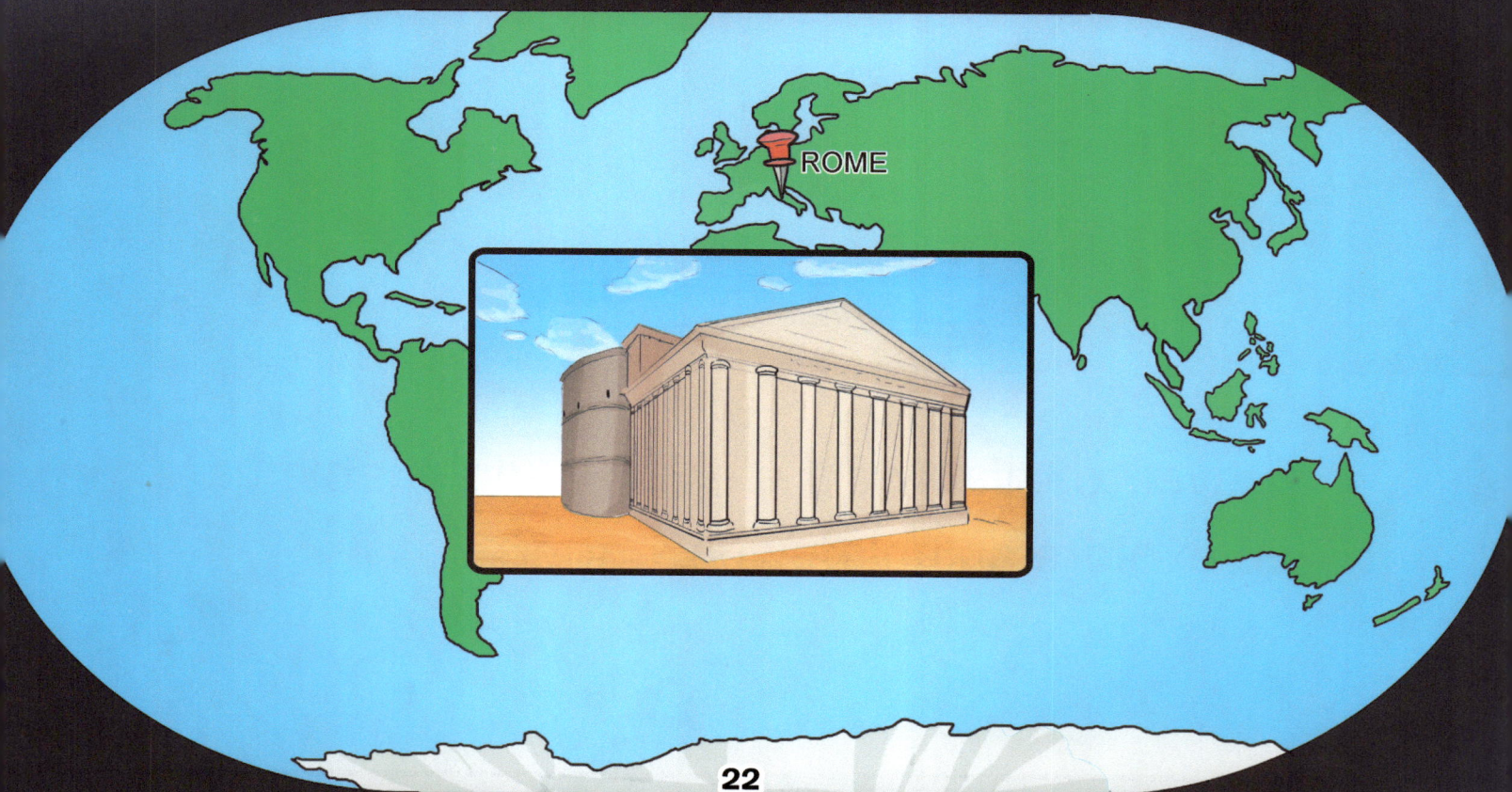

ROME

Could we consider the mysterious Makemake for our holiday next year?

This will be a great start to a budding astronomer's future career!

We could try to collect samples from this icy and rocky dwarf planet.

Then again, we'll be warmer atop Mt. Grey, viewing the beautiful Lake Janet!

NEW ZEALAND

Let's look at our majestic moon for our cosmic holiday next year!

The moon is certainly far closer than any planet out there might appear!

But with a single ticket costing millions or even billions this is one pricey short vacation!

Just like a ride in the orbiting laboratory known as the International Space Station.

A round-the-world trip would be far cheaper, even one taking in Earth's every nation!

Instead let's just visit an astronomical observatory for our holiday next year!

We can eat and drink as normal, so my dad can still enjoy a chilled beer!

We'll set off in our new cosy campervan perhaps for the Siding Spring Observatory near Coonabarabran.

Through telescopes, we'll explore the dark and starry skies so much better than with our naked eyes!

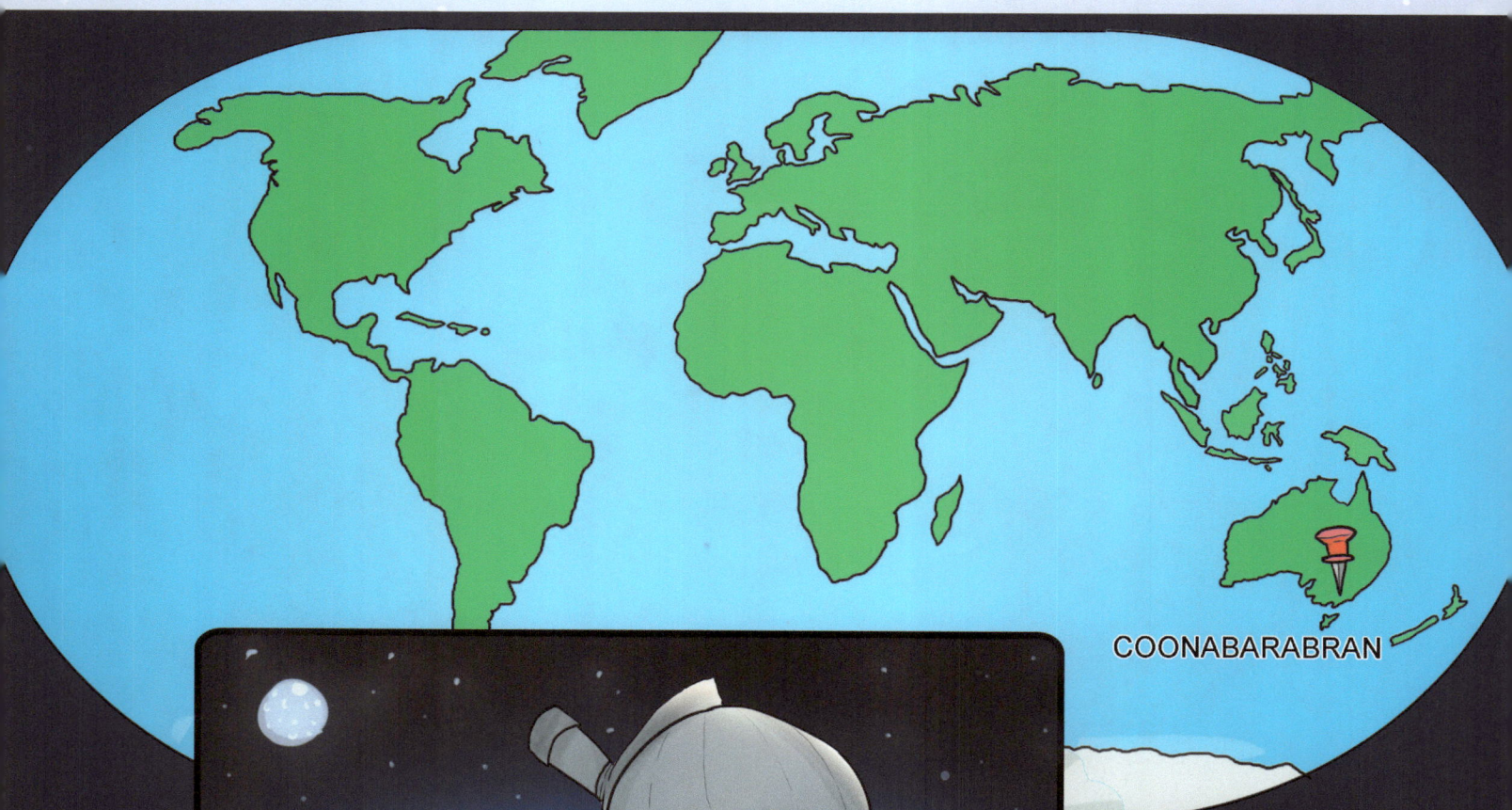

COONABARABRAN

28

So why can't we have an extraordinary holiday in space next year?

Because we can explore the beauty of our universe from right here!